Natasha ♡

The Angel Academy™ is a wonderful way to share morals and virtues with the children in your life. These stories, set in the endearing and whimsical Angel Heaven, allow children to learn life's most important lessons along with these fictitious guardian angels-in-training.

Presented to

_____

By

_____

On

_____

Trademark application has been filed on the following: The Angel Academy™, StarCentral™, Angel Heaven™, Jubilate™, Mirth™, Angelus™, Stella the Starduster™, Astrid™, Staria™, Miss Celestial™, Puffaluff™, Goodnight Hat™.

Managing Editor: Laura Minchew
Project Editor: Beverly Phillips

Art for The Angel Academy™ characters designed by Karen Bell.
Interior illustrations and front cover art designed by Dori McBride.
Cover illustrations by Karen Bell.
Interior illustrations and art assistance by Dori McBride • Guy Wolek
Kathleen Dunne • Betsy Rotunno • James Henry • Christine Tuveson
of Rosenthal Represents.

Library of Congress Cataloging-in-Publication Data

Taggart, Misty, 1940–
 The Angel Academy: a collection of modern angel tales / created and written by Misty Taggart;
 illustrated by Dori McBride
  p. cm.
 "Word kids!"
 Summary: The Angel Academy trains angels who come to earth to help children make moral choices and decisions.
 ISBN 0-8499-1161-3
 [1. Guardian angels—Fiction. 2. Angels—Fiction.] I. McBride, Dori. II. Title
PZ7.T1284An 1994
[E]—dc20   94-21206
                                                                    CIP
                                                                    AC

Printed in the United States of America
94 95 96 97 98 99 RRD 9 8 7 6 5 4 3 2 1

THE
ANGEL ACADEMY
A COLLECTION OF MODERN ANGEL TALES

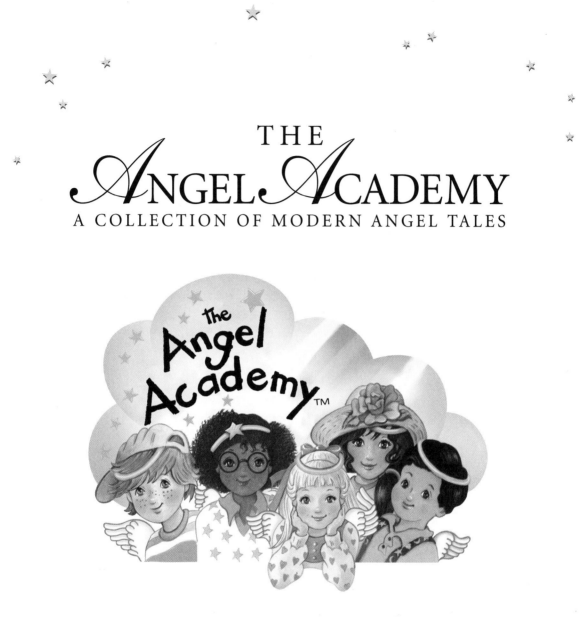

Created & Written by

MISTY TAGGART

WORD kids!®

WORD PUBLISHING
Dallas·London·Vancouver·Melbourne

For my Joe—
friend, husband, father,
and grandfather

In my heart is where the children play
No matter what their age today.
Memories of days now come and gone
Make room for the joys of a brand new dawn.

For Terry, Cara, Christopher,
Cody, Cassie, Louis, Dylan

❖ ❖ ❖

ACKNOWLEDGMENTS

There are so many people I wish to thank—too many to list in this space. But I especially thank Candy Monteiro and Fredda Rose who never lost faith in me or these angels-in-training. And to Bill Hanna, friend and mentor, who believed in the "little gal" who called him thirty years ago to say, "I want to be a writer."

Also, I thank the many friends who encouraged me. Finally, I would like to thank Laura Minchew who caught the vision of The Angel Academy and ran with it. And Beverly Phillips who brought her expert editor's eye to each page.

Contents

Behind the third cloud to the right,
just around the corner from the rainbow,
is The Angel Academy. This is where young angels
learn to be real guardian angels.

STARIA

She thinks she's very grown-up, but don't you believe it.

ASTRID

Her laugh is as big as her sweet tooth.

JUBILATE

He's ready to right every wrong—and has a lot of fun doing it.

ANGELUS

If you have a question about anything, he has the answer—he thinks.

MIRTH

She may be small, but she can be big trouble.

A Peek Around the Rainbow

$\mathcal{M}$irth and her pet cloud, Puffaluff, were outside the window at StarCentral. Jedediah, the angel in charge of Angel Heaven's information center, called to her.

"Vacation's over, Mirth! It's time for school."

"I'm not going!" said the little angel. Mirth was five and a half, and this was her first year at The Angel Academy.

"But you have to go to school to get your guardian angel wings," Jedediah reminded her.

"I don't care!" Mirth mumbled.

Jedediah had to go deliver an Earth Assignment. "See you later, Mirth. And don't forget, when The Angel Academy bells ring, all angels-in-training must go straight to school."

Jedediah had hardly gone, when the star on top of his computer began to *BLINK!*

"Look! It's another Earth Assignment! If I go to Earth, I won't have to go to school," Mirth said with a naughty giggle. "Come on, Puff!"

Mirth and Puffaluff took the Assignment and hurried off through Angel Heaven toward the Big Cloud Slide that reached all the way to Earth.

Mirth's best friends, Astrid, Angelus, Staria, and Jubilate, were also guardian angels-in-training. Going to The Angel Academy was nothing new to them. But school vacation was never long enough.

Astrid had spent her days testing new flavors at the Astroswirl Shop. Angelus had read a new book every day. Today they were both at the Astroswirl Shop.

"Chocolate whip with marshmallow stars and rainbow sprinkles is my very favorite," Astrid said, ordering another dish of astroswirl (astroswirl is like ice cream, only much better).

Just then, Astrid saw Mirth and Puffaluff rushing past the shop window. "Where are you going in such a hurry?" Astrid shouted.

But Mirth didn't stop to answer. Her Earth trip was a *big* secret. Everyone knew she wasn't supposed to go to Earth alone.

Not far away, Staria was walking through Cumulus Park picking wild flowers. She stopped to admire her reflection in the Daydream Pool just as Mirth ran past. "Wait, Mirth, I'll walk to school with you," Staria called.

"I'm not going to school!" Mirth giggled as she and Puffaluff disappeared around the corner of the rainbow.

The bells in The Angel Academy tower rang out. *DING! DONG! DING! DONG!* Angels-in-training from all over Angel Heaven hurried to their classes.

"Where's Mirth?" Jubilate asked Staria when she arrived at school. He, Angelus, and Astrid had been waiting for the little angel on The Angel Academy steps.

"I didn't believe her when she said she wasn't coming to school," said Staria.

Suddenly Jedediah burst through a cloud bank at top speed. He was looking for a misplaced Earth Assignment. "Where could it be?" he moaned. "I'm always so careful. I don't know how this happened."

"We haven't seen it. But have you seen Mirth? We've misplaced her, too!" declared Astrid.

Jedediah scratched his head. "Last time I saw Mirth, she and that sneaky cloud, Puffaluff, were floating around outside StarCentral!"

"StarCentral?" Angelus leaped into the air. "That's it! You know how much Mirth wants to go to Earth! I'll bet she took the Earth Assignment."

"But Mirth can't fly," exclaimed Jubilate. "Even if she took the Big Cloud Slide to Earth, she'd never be able to fly back home."

Staria was scared. "How would Mirth get back to Angel Heaven?" They all knew that if she stayed on Earth too long, her angel wings would disappear completely.

Mirth's friends were about to race off in search of her when they were stopped by Stella the Starduster. "Oh, no you don't! It's time for school."

"But Mirth's missing!" Staria called as she followed the others up the stairs.

"We'll find her!" Stella promised. Then she and Jedediah rushed off to search every corner of the clouds.

Mirth was peering over the edge of the Big Cloud Slide. It was a long way down to Earth, but anything was better than going to school. "I wish you could go with me, Puffaluff."

So did he. But Angel Heaven clouds could never go to Earth.

"Here goes!" Mirth closed her eyes tightly and jumped off the cloud.

Then, suddenly . . . she was caught up in midair!

"One minute, missy!" said Stella. "Where do you think you're going?"

Mirth gulped, "To school."

Meanwhile, school had barely gotten started and already Staria, Jubilate, Astrid, and Angelus were in the Archangel's office.

Staria had spent too much time daydreaming. Jubilate was tossing his sky disk instead of paying attention to the teacher. And Astrid had gotten in trouble for hiding cookies between the pages of her new schoolbooks.

"Not you, too, Angelus?" The Archangel was surprised to see that one of his smartest angels was in trouble.

"Angelus is a know-it-all. He thinks he's smarter than his teacher." The annoyed teacher threw up her hands and left.

"What am I going to do with all of you?" the bewildered Archangel moaned.

Outside the Archangel's office, a young and very beautiful guardian angel paced back and forth. Miss Celestial was unhappy. She had not been given a class to teach.

"Pardon me, but this angel-in-training is looking for a teacher," said Stella, gently pushing Mirth toward the startled teacher.

"Well, she's found one! Come with me," smiled Miss Celestial.

Miss Celestial flung open the door to the Archangel's office.

The funny sight inside made Mirth and Miss Celestial laugh. The office was a wreck. Jubilate's red sky disk was balancing on the poor Archangel's bald head!

When the guardian angels-in-training saw Mirth they all cheered.

The Archangel smiled with relief. His problem was solved. "Miss Celestial, . . . meet your new class!"

Mirth laughed. School might not be so bad after all!

Emperor of the Ice Palace

*S*hoo! Get away from that window, Puffaluff!" demanded Staria, trying to sound very grown-up. Staria was the oldest guardian angel-in-training in her Angel Academy class. And Miss Celestial had left her in charge for a few moments.

Puffaluff the Cloud was floating outside the window making funny shapes and faces. "You're so bossy, Staria," said Mirth, running to the window to play with Puffaluff. Jubilate joined her.

Astrid tossed a paper airplane at Puffaluff. "Besides, Miss Celestial will never know."

"Oh, really? . . ." said Miss Celestial. She had just returned.

"Oops!" exclaimed Jubilate. He and Mirth rushed back to their seats. Puffaluff gave the annoyed teacher a big, silly grin and quickly floated off.

Staria sighed, "They're such children."

"Staria thinks she's so big," Astrid whispered to Mirth. The two girls giggled.

On Earth, seven-year-old Cody Richards was sound asleep, snuggled in his warm bed. "Wake up, sleepyhead!" said his father.

Cody yawned, "But, it's Saturday."

"I guess you don't want to see your surprise!"

Cody was out of bed in an instant. "What is it? What is it?" he asked, jumping up and down.

His father smiled, pointing out the window. "See for yourself!"

Cody rushed to the window. "Wow!"

During the night, while everyone slept, the backyard had turned into a winter wonderland, covered with ice and snow. "Yea! It snowed!" He quickly dressed and ate breakfast so he could go out to play.

Cody and his two best friends, Maribelle and Benjamin, stood knee-deep in the crisp, new snow. They gazed with wonder at the old log clubhouse in Cody's backyard. "Look at that!" said Benjamin.

Maribelle gasped, "It's beautiful." Overnight, it had become a dazzling ice palace.

Shimmering icicles hung from the snow-covered roof. The frosted windows sparkled like beautiful jewels in the cold morning sunlight. Four nearby fir trees looked like towers guarding the palace.

"Come on! Let's go inside," cried Benjamin. He crunched through the snow, heading for the door. Maribelle stuck her sled in a snowbank and followed him.

Cody blocked the door. "You can't go in!" he said. Benjamin and Maribelle were surprised.

"It's my ice palace! I'm the Emperor!" announced Cody. "If you do what the Emperor says, maybe then I'll let you go inside."

"Aren't we friends anymore?" asked Benjamin.

"I'm the Emperor! I don't need friends," said Cody.

The Angel Academy class was interrupted by—
BLINK! TWINKLE! BLINK! TWINKLE! Miss Celestial's
StarCom pin started blinking!

"It's an Earth Assignment!" Jubilate shouted.
StarCentral had gotten word that an Earth child
needed angelic help. Earth Assignments are a very
important part of guardian-angel training.

Jedediah the Operator of StarCentral would be
bursting into the room any minute. "Stand back,"
Angelus said with a big grin.

As expected, the classroom door flew open.
Jedediah raced in. "There's big trouble at Cody's Ice
Palace!" he said, handing Miss Celestial the
assignment. "Hope you cherubs like snow!"

Staria said dreamily, "Oh, my! That means
snowballs and snowmen and—"

"Snow angels!" Astrid shouted. "What fun!" Angel
Heaven never had snow. So, every one of the angels-
in-training wanted this assignment.

But this time, Miss Celestial sent Angelus and Astrid.

Stella the Starduster stood beside the Big Cloud
Slide to Earth. "Wear these mittens and scarves,"
she said.

Angelus reminded her, "Angels don't feel the cold."
But they knew, if Stella said wear them, they'd better
do it. The guardian angel waved as Astrid and Angelus
jumped on the slide and disappeared into the clouds.

Meanwhile, Benjamin was shoveling a path to Cody's Ice Palace. And the Emperor was sitting on Maribelle's sled as she pushed it down the hill.

"This is fun!" giggled Cody. But it was easy to see Cody was the only one having fun. "The Emperor wants another ride!"

"I don't like this game," Maribelle said angrily.

"Me either! Let the *Emperor* shovel his own path," said Benjamin. "Come on, Maribelle! This isn't fun anymore."

"Go on! Who needs you anyway?" Cody called. It was his ice palace, and he could do whatever he pleased.

"Hi there, Emperor," said Angelus. Cody whirled around to find the two angels-in-training floating down through the snow-covered trees.

He blinked. He rubbed his eyes. "Who are you?" he said, completely stunned.

"I'm Angelus, and this is Astrid."

"Whee!" giggled Astrid, falling into a snowbank. She moved her arms and legs back and forth in the white flakes, making a snow angel.

Inside the ice palace,
Astrid told Cody they were here
to be his friends. "I've got friends," he said.

"You look a little lonely, if you ask me," Angelus
remarked.

Cody knew Angelus was right. Being Emperor of
the Ice Palace hadn't turned out to be much fun. He
missed Benjamin and Maribelle.

"Let's go find them," said Astrid. "Come on!"

But Cody would not budge. "No. They're the ones
who left."

This was one stubborn emperor. But if anyone
could figure out a way to get these three friends back
together, it would be Angelus.

"I've got it!" Angelus told Astrid. Then, leaving the
lonely emperor inside his ice palace, the two angels
flew off.

The guardian angels-in-training discovered Benjamin and Maribelle making a snowman. Maribelle didn't look very happy.

"Cody makes the best snowman faces," she said. Benjamin agreed. They missed their friend.

Suddenly, *SPLAT!* A big snowball hit Benjamin. "Hey!" *SPLOOSH!* Maribelle was the next target.

"Good shot, Astrid!" Angelus shouted, as the two angels kept throwing the snowballs.

The surprised children looked all around. But they couldn't see Angelus or Astrid. They were Cody's angels, and Cody was the only one who could see them.

Maribelle and Benjamin began to laugh. "It's a ghost attack!" Benjamin shouted. They began throwing snowballs at their unseen attackers. One of the snowballs hit Angelus. "It was just a lucky shot," Angelus said to Astrid. "This is fun!"

The angels' plan was working. Using the snowball fight, they were leading Maribelle and Benjamin back to Cody's clubhouse.

Cody heard the laughter and came out of his palace. "Hey, what's going on?" Before anyone could answer, *SPLAT!* A wet, cold snowball hit Cody's snow jacket.

"Go for it, Cody!" yelled Angelus.

Cody was happy to see Maribelle and Benjamin. He quickly joined the snowball fight.

"Thank you," he whispered to his angels. This was much more fun than being a lonely emperor.

When Cody's mother brought out warm cocoa for the children, she couldn't imagine why Cody wanted two extra cups. Cody just smiled.

The afternoon sun began to slowly melt the Emperor's Ice Palace. In no time, it would be Cody's old log clubhouse once again.

"I'm sorry I acted so bossy and didn't share," Cody told Maribelle and Benjamin. They forgave him. Good friends always do.

Angel in the Attic

*S*tella the Starduster was busily dusting and shining a cluster of twinkling stars in Angel Heaven. And George the Heavenly Handyman was adjusting the Big Cloud Slide to Earth.

Suddenly, George was almost knocked off his ladder as Jedediah the Operator of StarCentral came zooming past on his bicycle. Jedediah was waving an Earth Assignment in the air.

"Sorry," he shouted, "but there's an emergency at 703 North Jackson Street. A little girl is about to get into big trouble!"

41

That little girl was Amanda. She and her twin brother, Andy, were seven years old. They loved spending time with their Grandma Leta. Her big, old house was full of wonderful surprises—especially in the attic. Today Amanda and Andy were playing while Grandma Leta filled several rummage-sale boxes and took them downstairs.

"Do I look like Mommy?" Amanda giggled as she clumped around in a pair of old high heels, wearing a furry cape and a big, fancy hat.

"No. You look dumb," Andy replied.

"Who cares what you think," said Amanda, looking at her reflection in a large mirror.

Andy wore one of his Grandpa's old fishing hats that was covered with fishing hooks and flies. "I'm gonna catch a big one!" he exclaimed, as he hopped around trying to pull on a pair of huge rubber boots.

After a while, Amanda got bored and began searching for new treasures. "Oh, look!" she called, making her way through a stack of boxes. "It's a doll carriage."

From their classroom window in Angel Heaven, Miss Celestial and her class of guardian angels-in-training watched the Earth children play.

"Oh, what a lovely old doll," Staria said, as they saw Amanda take it from the carriage.

"The face is all cracked," remarked Jubilate.

Miss Celestial smiled. "But that doll once was as beautiful as Amanda's new doll."

"The new doll is a lot better," Astrid replied. "Nobody wants an old cracked one."

Miss Celestial decided this would be the perfect Earth Assignment for Astrid.

The guardian angel-in-training wasn't sure why Amanda would need her, but she never turned down an Earth Assignment.

Meanwhile on Earth, Andy lost interest in the attic and went downstairs. Amanda pulled the carriage out from its hiding place. "This will be perfect for my new doll," she said, tossing the old doll into one of the rummage-sale boxes. Then she hurried to the stairs.

"Hey, wait for me!" Astrid called.

Amanda was startled. She whirled around and saw her heavenly visitor. "Who are you?"

"I'm Astrid, from Angel Heaven."

"An angel? In Grandma's attic?" exclaimed Amanda. "Oh, wow!"

Amanda had found many wonderful things in Grandma Leta's attic, but never anything as wonderful as an angel.

"I want Grandma Leta to see you. Come on."

But just then her grandmother came up the stairs with two men from the church rummage sale.

"Those are the other boxes," Grandma Leta said, pointing to the boxes she had filled for them. It was then Amanda realized that her grandmother and the men couldn't see or hear Astrid.

Later that afternoon, Amanda and Astrid were in the front yard. Amanda hugged her beautiful, new doll. "I love her so much," she told Astrid.

"What's her name?" the angel asked.

"Lily," Amanda answered.

"That's a nice name," said Astrid. "Let's take Lily for a walk."

Amanda put her new doll in the old doll carriage. She proudly pushed Lily across the lawn and onto the sidewalk.

From the front porch, Grandma Leta called out, "Amanda, what are you doing with that doll carriage?"

Amanda explained that she had found it in the attic.

"Where is the doll that was inside the carriage?" her grandmother asked. She seemed worried.

"It was old and all cracked. So I put it in one of those boxes," said Amanda.

Well, it didn't take long for Grandma Leta to realize that the old doll must have been taken to the rummage sale. "Oh, dear!" she exclaimed. "Oh, dear me!"

Amanda couldn't
understand why her
grandma was so upset
about such an old doll.
Andy watched from the house.
He was glad to know that this time
he wasn't the one in trouble.

"Honey, that was your mother's first doll,"
Grandma Leta said. "She loved it very much."

"Uh-oh!" Now Astrid understood why Miss
Celestial had sent her to help Amanda.

"Does Mommy ever go to the attic to see her
doll?" Amanda asked.

"Yes, darling, I'm sure she does. After you have
Lily for a long, long time, you won't ever want to
lose her, either—even when you're all grown up."

Amanda felt terrible.

"Oh, Astrid, I just have to get my mother's doll
back. Come on!"

The little girl got permission from her grandmother to go down the street to the church rummage sale.

Andy came out of the house just in time to see Amanda running down the street with her new doll. Astrid was with her, but, of course, Andy couldn't see the angel because she was Amanda's angel-in-training. Andy decided to follow his sister.

People were already crowding into the church parking lot for the rummage sale. Furniture, clothing, and odds and ends were scattered everywhere. When Amanda saw all the boxes, she felt very sad. "Oh, Astrid, we'll never be able to find my mother's doll!" she cried.

"Yes we will!" said Astrid. She quickly started flying from box to box.

Andy ran up to his sister. "Look, Amanda!" He was pointing to a little girl who was holding tightly to their mother's old doll.

"I'll get her attention, then you grab the doll!" he said, running toward the little girl.

"Do you think I should do that?" Amanda asked her angel.

"No," Astrid said. The little girl looked so happy to have the old doll.

Andy finally gave up and started back to Grandma Leta's.

Amanda felt helpless.

"What should I do, Astrid?" she asked. "I have to get that doll back."

Astrid thought and thought. "I know, tell her it's broken and you'll help her find a better doll in another rummage-sale box."

"That might work," said Amanda. She walked over to the little girl. "Hi. That sure is an old doll. You don't really want her, do you?"

The little girl hugged the doll. "Oh yes, I do. I love her."

Amanda was sure she would not get the doll back. Then Astrid had an idea. She was certain Amanda wouldn't like it. And the angel was right.

Amanda didn't like Astrid's idea at all. But she wanted her mother's doll back, so she did what Astrid suggested. Then Amanda quickly ran down the street toward Grandma Leta's.

"Hey, wait for me!" called Astrid. The angel hurried to catch up with Amanda.

Andy yelled from up ahead, "You forgot Lily!"

"No, I didn't," said Amanda. Her eyes filled with tears. "She's not my doll anymore."

Astrid was very proud of Amanda. She had done the only thing she could do—she traded her new doll for her mother's old doll. She had given Lily away.

Now, when Amanda's mother went to the attic to sneak a peek at her old doll, it would be lying in the carriage where she left it so many years ago.

Astrid said, "You must love your mother very much. Giving up Lily was a wonderful thing for you to do."

Amanda looked up at her with big, sorrowful eyes and said, "Then why does it hurt so much?"

Stella the Starduster and George the Heavenly Handyman watched from the edge of a cloud bank. They always kept an eye on the little angels, just in case they needed their help.

"Doing the right thing isn't always easy," said Stella, as she wiped a tear from the corner of her eye.

"Now don't go getting all soggy, Stella," George grumbled—secretly taking a wipe at his own eyes.

When Astrid returned to The Angel Academy, Miss Celestial gave her a big hug. "I think from now on, Amanda will be a bit more careful with things that belong to others."

"I think we all will," said Astrid.

Little Angel Lost

*M*iss Celestial told Mirth over and over again, "Don't ever go to Earth by yourself. You could never fly home. Your wings are much too small."

"But I'm five and a half," Mirth pouted. "And I never have any fun."

That very day Mirth overheard Jedediah the Operator of StarCentral talking to Stella the Starduster. An Earth boy named Elijah needed angelic help in a hurry. Mirth knew the older angels-in-training were away on Earth Assignments.

Mirth thought for a moment. Then she fluttered her wings. "Miss Celestial must be wrong," she said. "My wings feel big enough to me." So, right then and there, Mirth decided to take the Big Cloud Slide to Earth all by herself. No one saw her leave Angel Heaven, not even Puffaluff the Cloud.

Angelic good fortune led the little guardian angel-in-training to Elijah's house. She found the young boy brokenhearted. "My dog, Milo, is lost," he told his little angel.

"I'm good at finding dogs," Mirth said, stretching the truth. She hoped Miss Celestial wasn't listening. But now that Mirth had come on her first Earth Assignment, she just had to complete it successfully. Elijah was depending on her.

59

"I'm glad you're here," the little boy said. He just knew if anyone could find Milo, an angel could.

But after searching throughout the whole neighborhood without finding Milo, Mirth was about to give up. Suddenly a large black and white ball of fur came racing down the street toward her.

"Yikes!" Mirth shouted. She ran as fast as she could toward Elijah's house. Looking back, she saw that the big ball of fur was gaining on her.

At the last minute, Mirth ducked into Elijah's play fort. The furry ball raced past her and leaped onto Elijah. "It's Milo!" he shouted. "You found my dog! Thanks, Mirth!"

Mirth slowly came out of the fort. "Sure, I knew it was Milo all the time." Mirth glanced toward Angel Heaven. "Well, I did," she insisted.

With her Earth Assignment completed, Mirth was ready to return to Angel Heaven. "Uh-oh," she said, when she found she could not fly. Mirth should have listened to Miss Celestial. *Her wings were much too small.* "What will I do?" Mirth's big blue eyes filled with tears.

Elijah felt terrible. After all, the little angel-in-training had come to Earth to find his lost dog. "Don't cry. I'll help you somehow," he said.

Mirth could tell Elijah loved her. She smiled, "I think your love will carry me back home."

If you want to help, too, just send your love to Mirth. Then help her find the way back to Angel Heaven.

Which path will lead Mirth back to Angel Heaven?

START

When Angels Smile

Staria was not at all happy. Astrid had been elected to represent Miss Celestial's class of guardian angels-in-training at The Angel Academy Spelling Bee.

"I should be going. After all, I *am* the oldest," Staria said, sticking her nose in the air.

"But you're not the best speller, Staria," said Astrid.

Staria replied, "You're just jealous because you're not as beautiful as I am."

Miss Celestial entered the room just in time to put a stop to this hurtful and unnecessary argument. "Staria, I'm surprised at you! Beauty isn't just how someone looks. Beauty comes from inside."

But, it was too late. Astrid's feelings had already been hurt by Staria's careless words. "I thought we were friends," Astrid said, as she ran from the room.

On Earth, six-year-old Jessica Duckworthy had made a big decision. Today, she didn't want to be a Duckworthy . . . because today a photographer was coming to take the family portrait. And this was one family get-together she was hoping to miss.

"He'll be here soon," said Mother. She wanted all six Duckworthys to look their very best.

The family lined up on the stairs for Mother's inspection. She straightened Father's tie, rebuttoned Jason's shirt, and combed Jeremy's hair. Then she helped Jennifer with her pretty orange hairbow.

Everyone looked just right. But where was Jessica? They were one Duckworthy short.

Father went to find Jessica. "Come on, sweetheart!" he called, as he came into her room.

But Jessica didn't answer. She held her breath and closed her eyes. Maybe, if she could be very, very quiet, no one would find her. But her father knew just where to look. She was, as usual, under her bed.

"Hi, honey," he said lovingly.

Her plan had failed. Reluctantly, Jessica squirmed out from under the bed. "I don't want to be in that old picture, Daddy."

"We couldn't have a family picture without you," he said, giving her a big hug. "Now, hurry and get ready!"

After a quick bath, Jessica stared at her reflection in the bathroom mirror. "Yuck!" she exclaimed. "I look goofy."

She just knew the rest of the family would look so nice—but not her. Her smile was crooked. And her glasses made her eyes look far too big for her face. Then there was the absolute worst thing of all—a gaping hole, right in the front of her smile. It was bad enough that she was missing two front teeth! And now they wanted her to let them take her picture.

"I just can't do it!" said Jessica, as her big eyes filled up with tears.

"Yes, you can. I'll help you," said an unfamiliar, but very lovely voice. It was Staria.

"YIKES! It's an angel!" Jessica exclaimed, seeing Staria's reflection in the mirror.

"If I were beautiful like you, I'd love having my picture taken," Jessica said. "Make me look like you, Staria."

"Let's try," said the little angel.

Jessica usually didn't wear dresses. But, at Staria's insistence, she wiggled into a pretty, pink, ruffled one. Staria rummaged through Jessica's closet, until she found an old, oversized gardening hat.

"This will have to do." Staria snipped some bright red geraniums from a pot outside the window and pinned one of them on the hat.

She added a ribbon to Jessica's unruly hair. Then the angel-in-training set the hat on the little girl's head, just so. "There! You're ready."

Jessica ran to the mirror. "Oh, dear," she cried, as the big hat with the geranium slipped down over her eyes. Both Jessica and Staria began to laugh. "Now I really do look funny," Jessica said.

She did look silly trying to be someone else. "Thanks anyway, Staria, but I'd rather look like me." Jessica tossed the hat aside, took the ribbon from her hair, and ran to join the rest of the family.

The Duckworthy family portrait was taken. And Staria flew back to Angel Heaven.

A few weeks later, Astrid and Mirth were trying to keep up with Staria as she hurried to The Angel Academy.

"I'm really sorry I hurt your feelings, Astrid," Staria said, as the three angels-in-training burst into Miss Celestial's classroom.

Then Staria rushed straight to the window that looked down on Earth. "Oh, Miss Celestial," she called, "you were right. It doesn't matter how you look on the outside. Come and see!"

They all peered through the clouds and saw Jessica and her father. The Duckworthy family portrait had finally arrived. As Jessica's father hung it on the wall, Staria held her breath.

Then, thankfully, Jessica giggled. "What's so funny?" asked her father.

"I am. But I like being me!"

Yes, Jessica saw her crooked smile and her very happy eyes that looked too big for her face. And there, as big as you please, was the hole where her two front teeth should be.

"Isn't she beautiful?" said Staria proudly.

Jessica smiled as she looked up toward Angel Heaven. She hoped her guardian angel-in-training could see how happy she was.

"Oh, look," Staria said. "Jessica's getting her two, new front teeth!"

Astrid and the others watched with excitement as Staria's wings grew the tiniest bit. In Angel Heaven, wings grow each time an angel-in-training successfully completes an Earth Assignment. And Staria's assignment had been a big success.

Perfect Penelope

Eight-year-old Penelope had been waiting a long time for just the right family to adopt her.

"Penelope needs a little angel help," said Jedediah the Operator of StarCentral in Angel Heaven. "She's going to visit the Poppenhagen family. And she's afraid they won't like her," he announced to Miss Celestial's class at The Angel Academy.

All the guardian angels-in-training wanted to help Penelope. But Miss Celestial chose only two. Angelus and Staria would make the trip from Angel Heaven to Earth.

"Come on, Angelus!" called Staria. She held onto her hat as she disappeared down the Big Cloud Slide to Earth. Angelus was right behind her. They slid around and around and around, down through layers of fluffy white clouds.

Meanwhile, Penelope was getting ready to go to the Poppenhagens' for the whole weekend. She thought to herself, *I have to be perfect.*

Then suddenly she remembered, "Uh-oh, I forgot to pack Pony." But when she ran to get her favorite stuffed toy, she was surprised to see two real live angels!

"Oh, my! Where did you come from?" she asked, looking a bit startled.

"Angel Heaven," answered Angelus. "We came to help you."

Staria smiled. "He's Angelus, and I'm Staria. We're going to the Poppenhagens' with you."

Penelope, Staria, and Angelus quickly became friends. The little girl was happy that her very own guardian angels-in-training would be with her at the Poppenhagens'.

Later, as her foster parents' car turned down Blossomwood Street, Penelope's heart raced faster. "This is just perfect," she whispered to her two angel companions. "Look at all these beautiful homes."

"What did you say, sweetheart?" asked her foster mother.

"Oh, nothing," giggled Penelope. What fun to have her very own angels that absolutely no one else could see or hear!

Penelope peered out the car window as they drove into a long driveway. They stopped in front of a lovely, brick house. Colorful flowers were in bloom everywhere.

Penelope was feeling a little frightened. She clutched her toy pony tightly. "Everything looks so perfect," she said to Staria. "I'm afraid they won't want me. I just know it. I'm not perfect enough."

Then the front door opened and out came Mr. and Mrs. Poppenhagen. Mr. Poppenhagen was very tall and thin with a mustache that twitched when he smiled. Mrs. Poppenhagen was short and round, and very happy to see Penelope. "Welcome!" they said. They looked so kind.

Peter, Pamela, and Patty Poppenhagen came running to the door. They were all neatly dressed in very nice clothes. "Hi, Penelope!" they shouted. "We're glad you're here," said Pamela.

Oh my, what a perfect family. I could never be perfect enough for them, thought Penelope. At that moment, she wanted to go back to the foster home. There, everyone loved her, even if she wasn't perfect.

"Show Penelope where to put her things, Pamela," said Mrs. Poppenhagen.

Pamela and Patty's room was clean and neat. Nothing was out of place at all.

"This is just too perfect," said Staria.

"Something's wrong here," replied Angelus.

"That's yours, Penelope," said Patty, pointing to a comfortable-looking bed. "Are you really going to come live with us forever?"

Pamela was embarrassed by her sister's question. "Don't mind her. Dinner will be ready soon, Penelope. We'll see you downstairs."

Pamela grabbed her little sister's hand and quickly headed for the door. Penelope turned to her angels-in-training and said, "Please help me to be absolutely perfect."

"No one is perfect," Angelus told her.

But Penelope wasn't so sure. The Poppenhagens all looked perfect to her.

It was wonderful to be sitting around the big dining table with a real family.

"Say please and thank you," said Angelus.

"And use your napkin," Staria reminded her.

All was going quite well, until Penelope reached for the salt. She was being so careful, but somehow her arm hit the milk glass . . . *OOPS!* Angelus tried to catch it, but it toppled over, splashing across the tablecloth.

"Oh, I'm sorry," said Penelope. Tears burned her eyes. The Poppenhagens certainly wouldn't want to keep her around for long.

"It's all right, dear," said Mrs. Poppenhagen, as she cleaned up the spill. "Accidents will happen."

Well, this would have to be the only accident Penelope had this whole weekend. She simply had to try harder. After dinner, Penelope went straight to bed.

When Penelope was fast asleep, Angelus said, "The Poppenhagens sure aren't much fun."

Staria agreed, then added, "They are so perfect, they're boring." The two angels-in-training busily made plans to help Penelope fit in.

The next morning, Penelope overheard Staria say, "We'll show the Poppenhagens how to have fun!"

"Oh, please don't cause trouble," pleaded Penelope.

"Angels-in-training never do that," giggled Staria.

Angelus disappeared into the backyard. Staria followed Penelope to the kitchen, where Mother, Pamela, and Patty were busily making breakfast. "Good morning," said Mother.

Before Penelope could answer, Staria
said, "We're about to have some fun!"

She began flying about the kitchen. First,
Staria caused the toast to start popping out of the
toaster—toast was flying in all directions.

"Look out!" shouted Patty. Since none of the
Poppenhagens could see the angels, they had no idea
what was happening.

Next the little angel squeezed extra soap into the
dishwater that Pamela was running—soap bubbles
billowed over the sink and into the kitchen. But that
wasn't all. Staria then switched Mother's mixer to
high—and it flung blueberry pancake batter all over
the three Poppenhagens.

"Oh no!" sighed Penelope, "This is terrible!"

In the backyard, Angelus was taking care of his part of the plan . . . *CRASH!* The baseball Mr. Poppenhagen and Peter had been tossing in a game of catch came flying through the kitchen window!

This wasn't at all the kind of thing Penelope expected from angels!

For a long moment, everyone just looked completely stunned. Big globs of pancake batter dripped from Mrs. Poppenhagen's nose. And a slice of burned toast sat atop her head. Pamela and Patty were almost covered by a mountain of soap bubbles. And Mr. Poppenhagen and Peter stared through the broken window at the calamity inside.

The two naughty angels held their breaths. Had they gone too far?

Then the entire Poppenhagen family started laughing! It was the heartiest laugh Penelope had ever heard. This was exactly what the angels wanted.

"I don't know what went wrong, but our big plan is ruined," chuckled Mrs. Poppenhagen.

"What big plan?" Penelope asked.

Then Peter spilled the beans. "We thought if we tried to be the perfect family, you would want to come and live here." But now, they could all stop pretending and go back to just being themselves.

Penelope was so happy. "I'm glad you're not perfect, because I'm not perfect either. I spill my milk all the time."

Mr. Poppenhagen smiled broadly. "Well, little one, there's nothing perfect around here, except our love. And we'd like to share that with you, Penelope."

Back in Angel Heaven, Angelus and Staria were giving a report about their Earth Assignment with the perfectly proper Poppenhagens.

While the class enjoyed hearing about the flying toast and the mountain of bubbles—the part they loved best was the happy ending. And they all decided, it's always best to be yourself.

Amaryllis Tells about Monsters

StarCentral had gotten word that six-year-old Luis was having trouble with his nine-year-old sister, Amaryllis. He needed a little heavenly help.

Miss Celestial had given out the Earth Assignment. Two of her guardian angels-in-training were on their way. And Luis was about to get a very big surprise.

Mirth pouted as she and Puffaluff watched Jubilate and Staria jump onto the Big Cloud Slide to Earth.

"See ya, Mirth," they called, as they disappeared into the clouds below.

Mirth just couldn't help herself. She called, "Wait for me! I'm going, too!" Then she jumped onto the Big Slide. "Wheeeeee!"

But her pet cloud, Puffaluff, quickly blocked her way. "Hey! Move, Puff!"

He shook his head no and refused to budge. You see, Puffaluff knew it was very dangerous for Mirth to go to Earth. Her wings were far too tiny to fly her back home to Angel Heaven.

But Mirth was five and a half, and she thought she could do just about anything. "I never have any fun," she whined as Puffaluff scooped her off the Cloud Slide. Mirth looked back longingly at the slide. "I'm going to go. You just wait and see." Surely her wings had grown since the last time she went to Earth without permission.

On Earth, the lights had already been turned out in Luis's room. He was supposed to be asleep. But instead, he was sitting on the floor with his big sister, Amaryllis. She was telling one of her scary stories and making a horrible, ghostly moaning sound! Amaryllis loved this part.

In the moonlight, Luis hugged his toy giraffe so tightly the stuffing was about to pop out.

"WOOooooo!" Amaryllis moaned even louder.

"YIKES!" Luis yelled, as he leaped into his bed and pulled the covers over his head.

"You're a little scaredy-cat," his sister teased.

Luis didn't uncover his head until he was sure Amaryllis was gone. But just as he did, Jubilate spoke up. "Hey, don't let her stories scare you."

"It's a ghost!" Luis grabbed his giraffe and dove back under the quilt.

"You scared him, Jubilate!" said Staria, disapprovingly.

Then she spoke softly. "Come on out, Luis. We're here to help you." Her voice was sweet and kind. But Luis was quite sure it was Amaryllis trying to trick him.

"No! I won't come out! Go away!"

"See what you've done, Jubilate! Now, he's frightened of angels," Staria sighed.

"Angels?" said Luis. His sister told stories about monsters and ghosts, but never about angels. Well, he simply had to take another look. Slowly, Luis peeked out from under the quilt.

He blinked. It was true. There were two little angels standing right beside his bed. And he didn't feel the least bit afraid.

Soon, Luis was convinced that Staria and Jubilate were indeed his very own guardian angels-in-training.

The next morning, as Amaryllis walked past the closed bathroom door, she thought she heard giggling and talking. She listened. "It's just Luis!" Amaryllis said out loud. He was talking to someone. But it couldn't be Mom or Dad. They were downstairs eating breakfast.

"*WOOoooooo!*" The spooky sound was coming from behind the door. A chill ran up her spine. But Amaryllis wasn't about to be fooled. She threw open the door. "Okay, Luis. I know it's you," she said.

But the bathroom was empty. Suddenly the faucet came on—thanks to Jubilate, whom Amaryllis could not see. "Oh, my!" she said. Then the lights went on and off all by themselves. But it was really Staria. Amaryllis went running from the room, calling, "Mom!"

Luis came out from behind the shower curtain where he had been hiding. He had made the spooky sound. But now he was laughing so hard he could barely speak. "She was . . . really . . . scared. Thanks."

Staria looked a bit concerned. "Maybe we shouldn't have done that."

"If it stops Amaryllis from scaring Luis, it was worth it," said Jubilate boldly.

Later that afternoon, Luis peered out the school-bus window at the darkening sky. The wind began to howl.

"This is monster weather," whispered Amaryllis, as they hopped off the bus at their corner. "You'd better be extra careful!"

There was a loud *CRACK!* of thunder in the distance, and Luis ran to the house, followed by his two angels.

"Mom!" Luis called, as he rushed up the steps. His mother would make everything all right. He threw open the door. "Mom!" But there was no answer. The house was empty. Luis was frightened.

"Don't worry. We're here with you," said Staria.

Just as the thunder *CRACKED!* again, Amaryllis jumped out from behind a big armchair. "BOOOOO!" she shouted, and then she ran up the stairs, laughing.

Staria and Luis grabbed hold of Jubilate.

"Hey, don't let her scare you," Jubilate said. "Or she won't ever stop telling those monster stories."

Staria stepped back and straightened her hat. She tried to look calm. "Well . . . she certainly didn't scare me."

"I'm sure your mother will be back any minute," said Staria. She poured each of them a glass of milk. Luis got out some homemade gingersnaps.

Outside, the storm was getting worse. Branches of a nearby tree kept *KNOCK-KNOCKING* at the window.

"I think I'll call my grandma," Luis said. He tried, but the phone wasn't working.

"Don't worry," said Jubilate. "It's just the wind."

Luis tried to forget about the storm. "Why does Amaryllis want to scare me all the time?" he asked his angels-in-training.

"She just wants to let you know she's the oldest," said Staria.

Luis tried not to be frightened, but his sister's stories were scary. Suddenly, they heard a scream.

"It's Amaryllis!" Staria exclaimed.

But Luis didn't budge. "This time she's not going to trick me."

"Good for you," said Jubilate proudly.

Luis grabbed two more gingersnaps and dunked them into his milk.

"But Amaryllis sounded really frightened," said Staria. "Maybe we should just go make sure."

With the encouragement of his angels, Luis thought maybe he was ready to show Amaryllis she couldn't scare him—not anymore.

So, together, the three went up the stairs.

They peeked into his sister's room. There was Amaryllis standing on top of her bed, clutching her rag doll. She was terrified!

"There's a monster in my closet, Luis!" she shrieked.

"Stop making up monster stories," Luis said. "You're just trying to scare me. And it won't work anymore."

"But it's true this time! Really!" she said.

Then they heard *THUD-THUDDING!* sounds coming from her closet.

"See, there's something in there!" shouted Amaryllis.

Luis's eyes grew as big as saucers. "It is a monster!" he exclaimed. The noise grew louder as the monster thrashed about! Any minute it would burst out of the closet and grab them all! Luis and Staria looked at Jubilate for encouragement.

"Jubilate, are you . . . absolutely sure . . . there's no such thing as monsters?" asked a shaky Staria.

Jubilate stood his ground—but his stomach did a flippity-flop. "I'm . . . pretty sure. Whatever it is, it just can't be a monster."

Amaryllis hopped off the bed. "Luis, let's get out of here! I'm so sorry. I wish I'd never told those stories. Now they're coming true. We do have monsters!" She turned and ran out of the room. "Luis, get out of there!"

Suddenly, the closet door flew open! The lightning *FLASHED!*

Luis, Jubilate, and Staria grabbed hold of each other. They watched as something came out of the darkness. It was—*a pile of walking clothes.*

"Somebody help me!" The little voice was coming from inside the clothes. "Help!"

"It is a monster! Amaryllis was right!" cried Luis.

"Hold it, Luis!" Jubilate said. Then he and Staria began laughing. "That's no monster, that's Mirth!" giggled Staria.

They dug the little angel-in-training out from under the pile of clothing. Luis was amazed to see another angel.

Staria shook her head, "Mirth, you're going to be in *big* trouble when you get back to the Academy."

"I don't care," said Mirth. "I wanted to help."

Amaryllis peeked back into the bedroom. "Mother's home," she said with relief. Their mother had left a note on the door saying she'd be late, but the windstorm had blown it off.

Amaryllis spotted the big pile of clothing. "You scared away the monster! Oh, Luis, I won't ever tell those terrible stories again. I promise." And she ran to tell their mother about how brave Luis had been.

Luis smiled. The little angel 'ghost' had done her job.

"Don't let Mirth get into *too* much trouble," he said.

"We'll tell Miss Celestial how she 'accidentally' took care of your problem with Amaryllis," said Jubilate.

"It was so much fun," Mirth grinned.

"Good-bye," Staria called, as she and Jubilate flew out the window. Mirth fluttered her little wings as fast as she could—but as her friends expected, she just couldn't fly. "Wait for me!" Mirth called, a bit worried. Mirth knew she should not have disobeyed Miss Celestial again. Then, Jubilate swooped back and took Mirth by the hand.

"Oh, thank you," Mirth said. She was very, very lucky her friends were there this time to take her back home to Angel Heaven.

Luis waved good-bye to his angels. He knew they would be watching over him, and that made Luis feel very safe and very special.

Come to the Fair!

*I*t was time for the big State Fair. What fun! Emily had looked forward to this day all year. She jumped out of bed very early, dressed, and ate her breakfast. "Let's go, Daddy!" she said, pulling her father toward the door.

He looked very worried. "Honey, I'm so sorry, but I can't find our tickets." Everyone was disappointed. Emily's family did not have much money. So, without those tickets, they would not be going to the fair this year.

"Come on, everybody. We just have to find those tickets," Emily cried. And the entire family joined the search.

StarCentral was alerted. Emily needed help. Quickly, Jedediah headed for The Angel Academy with the urgent Earth Assignment.

When Jubilate heard the words *State Fair,* he jumped right out of his desk. "I'll go!" he shouted. "And when I find those tickets, I'm going to the fair, too!"

The guardian angel-in-training ran to the Big Cloud Slide to Earth. "So long!" he called to his classmates, as he disappeared into the clouds below.

Later on Earth . . .

"Who's under there?" Emily asked. She was very surprised to discover an angel-in-training under her bed.

"I'm your guardian angel-in-training. And I was looking for those missing tickets," Jubilate said. The two quickly became friends, and together they continued the search. They rummaged through all the closets and even inside Dad's toolshed. By then, the rest of the family had given up.

The last place Emily and Jubilate looked was in the basement. Emily's mother was about to wash a pile of shirts. Suddenly, Jubilate spotted something in one of Dad's shirt pockets. "Hey, there they are!" Jubilate shouted. Emily stopped her mother just in time to save the State Fair tickets.

So that day, Emily, her family, and Jubilate went to the fair after all.

"Hi, Emily!" Jubilate shouted, as he waved his baseball cap from the top of the Ferris wheel.

Some Earth Assignments were just more fun than the others.

Can you find these hidden things in the picture of the fair?

tickets	cotton candy	clown
baseball	dog	teddy bear
baby chicken	book	rabbit
scissors	hair brush	color crayon
halo	pie	cake
cookie	banana	butterfly
heart	snow cone	pencil

Kristina's Goodnight Hat

After six-year-old Kristina said her prayers, her mother tucked her into bed and softly kissed her forehead. "Goodnight, honey. Sweet dreams."

But Kristina didn't want to go to sleep. Lately her dreams hadn't been very sweet at all. That's why she had decided to stay awake all night. She did try. But soon her big, blue eyes closed, and she was fast asleep.

Word of Kristina's bad dreams had reached Angel Heaven. Miss Celestial sent Astrid on this Earth Assignment.

"I'll do my best," promised Astrid.

In the flutter of a wing, the guardian angel-in-training was sitting on top of Kristina's toy box. She watched the little girl sleeping. Kristina was tossing and turning.

Astrid noticed a toy piano. She loved music, and she was certain a lullaby would help Kristina sleep more peacefully. The angel began to play the piano softly.

But, what Astrid didn't know was that the toy piano had a broken key. When it was struck, it made the most terrible, off-key *TWANG!* Well, she hit that key. And the *TWANG!* woke Kristina, who sat straight-up in bed.

Kristina was startled to find an angel in her room. "Oh dear, I'm still dreaming!"

"No, you're not. I'm really here," Astrid assured her.

Astrid explained that she was the little girl's very own guardian angel-in-training. And Kristina soon discovered she was the only one who could see or hear Astrid. "This is going to be lots of fun," she told the angel.

The two new friends whispered under the covers. Astrid listened while Kristina talked about her bad dreams. The angel thought she knew what was causing the scary dreams.

"Maybe it's because your parents are going out of town tomorrow. But you don't have to worry, Kristina. I'll be with you. And so will Mrs. Butler." Mrs. Butler was the little girl's favorite babysitter.

It was getting very late. Kristina was sleepy. "Will you play that song again, Astrid?" the little girl yawned. Astrid began to play the lullaby on the toy piano, being careful to miss the broken key.

The angel and her Earth child slept peacefully all night.

The next day, Kristina took Astrid downstairs to the most wondrous place. It was a candy shop, and Kristina's father was the owner.

"Now, *I'm* dreaming!" Astrid said. "This must be candy heaven!" There were candy balls, candy sticks, and candy bars . . . and chocolate everywhere!

The angel was just about to sample some colorful jelly beans, when the candy jar was suddenly snatched up. "Hey!" Astrid shouted.

Clarissa Tweedie was busily dusting and rearranging the jars. Of course, she hadn't seen or heard Astrid. "Good morning, Kristina. Did you come to help me?"

"No, I was just . . . looking for my dad," smiled Kristina, remembering the woman couldn't see Astrid. Kristina's father had hired Clarissa to run his candy shop while he was away. Kristina and Astrid giggled about Clarissa's funny-looking hat. And they wondered what she carried in her big bag.

"I'd love to see what's inside," said Astrid.

Then Kristina's mother called, "Honey, Mrs. Butler's here. We've got to go."

With her favorite babysitter and her own guardian angel-in-training, Kristina bravely waved good-bye to her mother and father.

That evening, Mrs. Butler made a marvelous dinner. Kristina shared her bowl of delicious banana pudding with Astrid. It was all gone in a flash. Mrs. Butler was astonished when Kristina asked for another helping. "You certainly do love my 'nanna' pudding don't you?" she said, scooping up another big spoonful for the little girl.

Astrid said, "Thank you," even though the woman couldn't hear her.

Just then, the telephone rang, and Mrs. Butler hurried to answer it.

"I've closed the shop," said Clarissa Tweedie, peeking in the kitchen door. "Just wanted to say goodnight."

Clarissa reminded Astrid of someone in Angel Heaven. But who?

Mrs. Butler came back into the room. "Oh, dear. Something dreadful's happened. My husband is ill and I must go see about him."

Clarissa said she'd be happy to stay with Kristina.

Mrs. Butler called Kristina's mother and everyone agreed. It was a good plan.

Now, perhaps the little girl and her angel-in-training could find out just what Clarissa Tweedie kept in her very big bag.

They didn't have to wait long. At bath time, Clarissa opened it and pulled out the most bubbly bubble-bath soap Kristina had ever used. Later, from the mysterious bag came Kristina's favorite game, and Clarissa and Kristina played until bedtime. Astrid watched as Clarissa dug way down into the bag and found two of Kristina's favorite cookies—chocolate chip and peanut butter.

Astrid was beginning to think she wasn't needed at all—until it was time for Kristina to go to bed.

"Have a sweet-dream night," said Clarissa Tweedie, as she tucked Kristina into bed. She turned on a small angel night-light and tiptoed out of the room.

"I'm so glad you're here, Astrid," Kristina yawned. Then she suddenly giggled, "I wonder if Clarissa Tweedie sleeps in that hat?"

The little angel watched over Kristina until she was fast asleep. After that, Astrid couldn't think of anything except the candy shop, right downstairs. *"Kristina did say I could have whatever I wanted,"* Astrid said to herself.

In the candy store, the guardian angel-in-training sampled bonbons, peanut brittle, chocolate drops, and fudge. Then she popped a few gumdrops into her pockets for good measure. Now, Astrid would surely have 'sweet' dreams, too.

Back in Kristina's bedroom, Astrid was soon fast asleep. But her dreams were certainly not sweet. She dreamed that six very scary lollipops were chasing her around the room! And bonbon creatures crept up the walls and across the floor.

"Help!" Astrid screamed, waking herself up.

Her scream also woke Kristina, who was having her own bad dream. The little girl cried out, too, and Clarissa rushed into the room. "Tomorrow, we will shoo away these bad dreams," Clarissa promised Kristina. Both Kristina and Astrid giggled when they saw that Clarissa Tweedie was indeed still wearing her hat.

The next morning, before opening the candy shop, Clarissa took a very plain hat from her amazing, big bag.

"We're going to make you a *goodnight hat!*" she told Kristina.

"What is that?" Kristina whispered to Astrid.

"I don't know." But if a goodnight hat would chase away bad dreams, they both wanted one.

Clarissa and the little girl had fun going throughout the apartment looking for decorations to go on the special hat. Astrid followed them, wishing she could help.

Seeing a small package of golden glitter, Clarissa said, "Oh, that will be perfect." Then they gathered up shiny, old, mismatched buttons, colorful pieces of cloth, and just about anything you would NEVER think of using on a hat.

Then, Kristina and Astrid watched in amazement as Clarissa added each of the newfound treasures to the plain, little hat. Her needle and thread quickly darted in and out. Then . . .

There it was! The most wonderful hat the little girl had ever seen. Clarissa placed it on Kristina's head—it fit perfectly!

"Oh, thank you," said Kristina, admiring her hat in a mirror. Astrid wished she had one, too.

Immediately Clarissa Tweedie reached into her big bag again. And with a wink, she pulled out another splendid goodnight hat—almost as if she knew what the little angel was wishing. "Kristina, you just might need two of these," she said.

Now, Astrid would have her very own goodnight hat, after all.

That night, Kristina was actually looking forward to bedtime. She could hardly wait to put on her goodnight hat.

After Kristina's bath and her prayers, Clarissa made sure the goodnight hat was snugly in place. "When you're wearing such a lovely hat, how could you have anything but lovely dreams?"

Later that night when Kristina's parents returned, they peeked in on her. She was fast asleep. And her dreams were as sweet and lovely as her goodnight hat.

When Astrid returned to Angel Heaven, she took her goodnight hat with her. Not that she ever had bad dreams there—but, one day, she might eat just a little too much astroswirl.

"What a delightful hat, Astrid," said Stella the Starduster. "I do wish I had one as special as that in my hat collection."

Astrid smiled, thinking Stella looked a lot like Clarissa Tweedie. "I think it should be in your collection. But if I ever need it . . ."

"Your *goodnight hat* will always be waiting for you," Stella assured her.

"How did you know it was a goodnight hat?"

Stella smiled, "Angels just know."

Astrid peeked over the edge of a cloud and whispered, "Sweet dreams, Kristina."

An Angel Secret

The following story is a rebus story. It uses pictures for some words. Read the story and when you see a picture, use the correct word.

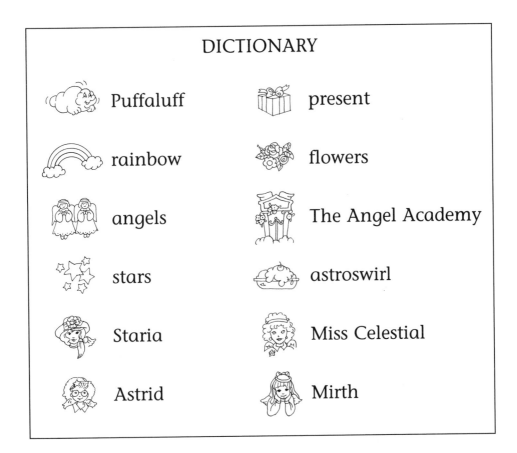

DICTIONARY

Puffaluff		present	
rainbow		flowers	
angels		The Angel Academy	
stars		astroswirl	
Staria		Miss Celestial	
Astrid		Mirth	

's guardian -in-training were rushing around Angel Heaven. And they had a very big secret!

"Now, what are those up to?" asked Stella the Starduster. She and George the Heavenly Handyman were dusting and hanging a cluster of glittering .

waved as she flew by on , her pet cloud. "Hurry, Puff. We don't want to be late." But grabbed George's halo and threw it into the air. The halo caught on the point of a star just above the . Quickly George went flying after his halo. But before he could reach it, the halo slipped off the star and fell into the clouds below. It was rolling toward , who was hurrying along with a giant-size dish of chocolate-meteor .

stepped from behind the just in time to stop . "Look out!" she shouted. One more step and her friend would have tripped over the halo and spilled the , ruining their surprise.

"Having a secret is so much fun," 🎀 giggled. The two friends rushed toward 🏛️ . When they arrived, Jubilate and Angelus were carefully carrying a very big 🎁 into their classroom.

Quickly the angels decorated the room with 🌹 . When 👧 arrived, all the 👼👼-in-training jumped out and shouted, "SURPRISE!" Then the 🎁 popped open, releasing a puff of twinkling stardust. 👒 smiled when she saw that the 🎁 was a string of golden ⭐ . Across the ⭐ were the words, FOR OUR FAVORITE TEACHER.

"Oh, thank you," said 👒 , as she hugged each of the little 👼👼-in-training.

"And you're my favorite 👼👼 at 🏛️ ."

Then they all laughed and ate big scoops of delicious 🍨 .

Everyone had a wonderful time, even 🐑 .

Once Upon a Cloud

The Angel Academy school day was almost over. It was very hard for the class of guardian angels-in-training to keep their minds on their studies. As soon as the bell rang, they would be going to Cumulus Park to play.

As he folded his Earth-science paper into an airplane, Jubilate was thinking about all the fun he would have after school. "Blast off!" Jubilate said quietly, sending the paper airplane through the air toward Staria's hat.

"Duck, Staria!" whispered Astrid. Staria ducked just in time.

Miss Celestial was writing tomorrow's assignment on the blackboard. Just then the Archangel entered the classroom for a visit. He saw Jubilate's paper airplane sail into the back of Miss Celestial's head.

"Uh-oh," exclaimed Jubilate, as he covered his eyes with his left hand. All the other angels-in-training gasped in horror!

"And what is this?" The Archangel asked, picking up the paper airplane. The principal didn't look a bit happy. Neither did Miss Celestial.

"Good afternoon, sir," she said. Oh, how Miss Celestial wished the Archangel hadn't seen her class misbehaving. "I'm afraid they thought the bell had rung," she said.

Just then, the bell did ring. But not one of the angels-in-training moved. They knew what was coming next. Miss Celestial was about to say, "You will all be staying after school today."

The whole class glared at Jubilate. "I'm sorry," he gulped.

The class did stay after school. They cleaned erasers, restacked books, and wiped the blackboards. Miss Celestial finally said, "Class dismissed." And the angels-in-training rushed through the clouds to Cumulus Park.

The Park was full of happy, laughing angels. Some of the cherubs were swimming in Daydream Pool. Others swung so high they almost touched the stars. One angel after another zipped past on cloud slides.

"I don't feel much like having a good time," said Jubilate. Neither did his classmates. They were sorry they had disappointed Miss Celestial.

"Hey, why all the sour faces?" called Stella the Starduster. She and George the Heavenly Handyman were planting a new, cloud flower garden in the park.

"Miss Celestial kept us all after school," said Astrid.

Then Angelus told the two grown-up guardian angels about the Archangel and the paper airplane.

"I guess when Miss Celestial was an angel-in-training, she was Miss Perfect," said Jubilate.

"Celestial? Oh, dear me, no," laughed Stella. "Celestial and Jedediah used to race through the clouds, playing hide-and-seek around the rainbow. Isn't that right, George?"

George nodded his head and smiled. "Troublemakers, both of them."

"Miss Celestial and Jedediah?" Staria couldn't believe it.

"Troublemakers?" Astrid thought that was impossible.

Stella sat down in the shade of a large weeping willow. "Come, sit beside me and I'll tell you a story." Quickly, the angels-in-training found places to sit. Even Puffaluff wanted to hear this story.

"Once upon a cloud," Stella began, "it was a particularly cloud-filled day in Angel Heaven. Celestial was about eight and Jedediah was nine or so. Well, these two angels-in-training were tearing around on Jedediah's bicycle. . . ."

"Hold on, Celestial!" Jedediah shouted. He was pedaling as fast as he could, and she was seated in front of him. Together, they recklessly burst through one cloud bank after another.

"Wow! This is more exciting than flying," Celestial giggled.

Now, if they had known what was just on the other side of the very next cloud bank, they most certainly would have slowed down—or avoided it completely. But instead, Jedediah pedaled faster and Celestial giggled louder.

They hit the cloud bank . . . and the Archangel! And before they knew what had happened, the poor Archangel was flying in one direction and his briefcase and books in the other.

"YIKES!" yelled Jedediah, as his bicycle spilled the two young angels onto the cloud. The stunned Archangel moaned, "Not you two again!" This was not the first time something like this had happened. Celestial and Jedediah were forever getting into some kind of trouble.

The Archangel found his glasses and slowly got to his feet. "Celestial, you and Jedediah are grounded for the rest of the semester. No more Earth Assignments for you!"

Stella smiled and said, "From that day on Celestial and Jedediah were much more careful."

"I guess Miss Celestial does know how we feel," said Jubilate.

"She just wants you to do the very best you can so you will be the best guardian angels ever," said George. "And she wants this because she loves you."

Mirth looked puzzled. "Miss Celestial kept us after school because she loves us?"

"That's right," answered Miss Celestial. The young angels were surprised to see their teacher riding up on Jedediah's bicycle. "Thanks, Jedediah. It was as much fun as it used to be," said Miss Celestial.

"Give me a ride, Jedediah! Please," begged Astrid.

"No, me first!" called Jubilate. "Let's go cloud-bank busting!"

"And how did you know about that?" asked Miss Celestial, giving a wink in Stella's direction.

They all laughed. These five guardian angels-in-training were so happy to have such a wonderful teacher. And the most wonderful thing was, they would all be together for a long, long time.

Look for these ANGEL ACADEMY™ books and products

at your favorite bookstore, gift shop, and retailer:

Sister, Stay Out!

Angel Parade Pileup

The Razzleberry Rescue

The Angel Academy Poster
by American Arts and Graphics
(23" x 35")

The Angel Academy:
A Collection of Modern
Angel Tales

Don't miss the fun! Join THE ANGEL ACADEMY™ KIDS CLUB.

A one-year membership includes a Welcome Packet of fun sent directly from Angel Heaven. You'll get a Club Membership I.D. Card, Angel Academy Surprises and Special Offers throughout the year, and a special Birthday Surprise!

Do not tear out this page from your book. Photocopy the form below or use a clean sheet of paper and PRINT the following information:

Child's Name: _____ Girl ❑ Boy ❑

Address: _____

City: _____ State: _____ ZIP: _____

Phone: (_____) _____ Age: _____ Birthdate: _____

For a one-year membership, send the completed registration form along with a check or money order for $10.00, per child, ($13.00 in Canada) to:

THE ANGEL ACADEMY™ KIDS CLUB
P.O. Box 39480
Membership Dept.
Phoenix, AZ 85069–9480

Please allow 6–8 weeks for delivery. Subject to change without notice. AZ residents add sales tax.